Contents

Disney PRINCESS

Tangled

Ghosts of Christmas Past

It should have been a joyous time. Christmas was coming – Rapunzel's very first Christmas since returning home to the castle. For the past 16 years of her life, she had spent every Christmas locked away in Mother Gothel's tower.

The castle halls were decked with boughs of holly. The butlers had just chosen the royal Christmas tree. Everyone was doing their best to spread holiday cheer. Even the grumpiest townsfolk were merry.

But in the royal family, one person was not ready for a happy holiday.

"No way. Uh-uh," said Rapunzel. "I refuse to celebrate Christmas."

"What?" cried Flynn. "Why don't you want to celebrate the most wonderful holiday of the year?"

Rapunzel looked shocked. "Wonderful?" she said. "I think you mean 'terrifying'!"

Flynn was confused – until Rapunzel shared her memories of Christmases spent in Mother Gothel's tower.

"You know how it is," Rapunzel said. "There's all of that eerie Christmas music. Mother Gothel sang it nonstop at Christmas time. I hate chanting and growling."

That didn't sound like any Christmas music Flynn had ever heard.

"Okay," he said, trying not to smile. "What else?"

"Mother Gothel also told us the tale of Nicholas, the ghostly Christmas elf – how he creeps into children's rooms on Christmas Eve and steals them away. It kept me up at bedtime!" Rapunzel sighed and shrugged. "But I guess that's why all kids have trouble sleeping on Christmas Eve. Didn't you?"

"Actually, no," Flynn said. "I couldn't wait to go to bed and wake up on Christmas morning. You know, that's not what Christmas is like at all."

From everything Rapunzel was telling him, he could see that Mother Gothel had gone out of her way to ruin Christmas for Rapunzel.

She didn't want Rapunzel to leave the tower, Flynn thought. *Ever.*

Well, he could do something to change things now!

Flynn smiled, taking Rapunzel by the hand. "You know what?" he said. "I'll show you what Christmas is really like. Come on!"

He led Rapunzel outside the castle. She kept close by his side, but Flynn reassured her. "Just look around – and listen," he said. "Does this seem like a spooky holiday to you?"

They passed a group of children singing Christmas carols. The harmonies were sweet and soothing. The verses were all about hope and joy. It was like no Christmas music Rapunzel had ever heard before.

A small boy raced over to Rapunzel. He held out a package wrapped with a golden bow. "Merry Christmas, Princess Rapunzel!" he said. "I made this especially for you!" But Rapunzel could only stare at the gift, her eyes wide as she started to back away.

"Trick package! Duck!" she cried, diving for cover behind a low stone wall.

She peeked out warily from her hiding place. Flynn and the children stared at her. Who ran away from a Christmas present?

"It's not a trick," Flynn said gently. "Just a gift."

He opened the box. Inside was a handwoven crown of evergreens.

Slowly, Rapunzel stepped out from behind the wall and took the crown from Flynn. She placed it on her head.

"A real Christmas gift?" she said, as if she'd never heard of such a thing. "Not an exploding trick package?" She kneeled by the little boy and took his hands in hers. "Thank you."

Rapunzel and Flynn wandered further into the town and came across a tree-trimming party. Together, the townsfolk were decorating an enormous Christmas tree in the town square.

Rapunzel pointed towards the top of the tree. "You need a lot more charms up there," she said, "if you want to scare off the ghostly Christmas elf." She picked up one of the ornaments. "And I'm not sure these charms are anywhere near scary enough."

Flynn took her aside. "They're not charms," he explained. "They're ornaments. For decoration."

Rapunzel frowned. "Oh. Well, then, how do you keep the Christmas elf away?"

Flynn couldn't help laughing. "Okay, next lesson."

They went back inside the castle, where Flynn found some books about the real St Nicholas.

"Oh! We had this one at the orphanage," Flynn said, holding up a blue book. "See, St. Nicholas isn't a ghostly Christmas elf. He's a jolly old fellow who travels far and wide on Christmas Eve, bringing gifts to all the boys and girls."

Flynn showed Rapunzel drawings of a smiling bearded man carrying a sack full of presents. "Definitely no kidnapping."

Rapunzel and her chameleon, Pascal, looked at each other. Rapunzel didn't know which of them was more surprised. To think of all those Christmas Eves they'd spent huddled together by the fire, too afraid to sleep! "You mean, children have trouble sleeping on Christmas Eve because they are *excited*?" she asked.

Flynn nodded. "That's right," he said. "Most children can't wait for Christmas." He watched Rapunzel take it all in. "So, now that you know what this festive time is really like, do you think you might be interested in celebrating it this year? For real? For the first time?"

Rapunzel's face lit up. "Yes!" she replied, and she sprang into action.

For the next few weeks, Rapunzel lived and breathed Christmas, enjoying everything that the holiday season had to offer – everything she had missed out on while living in the tower.

In the castle kitchen, she helped bake dozens and dozens of crumbly Christmas cookies.

She learned every word of every Christmas carol she had never heard before.

She decked every undecked part of the hall with garlands and ribbon, and for the first time, she made beautiful – not spooky – Christmas ornaments.

Finally, she brought together paper and ribbons and gift tags and carefully wrapped handmade gifts for each member of her family. She could hardly wait until Christmas to see them opened.

By the time Christmas Eve arrived, Rapunzel was exhausted, but very, very happy. Every room in the castle had been decorated with garlands and tinsel and presents were piled up beneath the Christmas tree, where her family gathered to celebrate.

Rapunzel's father, the King, proposed a toast. "For years, our hearts have not felt entirely whole at this time of year." He paused. "An important part of them was missing." He smiled at Rapunzel.

The Queen raised her golden goblet and added her own words to the toast. "But now, for the first time since you were born, Rapunzel, this holiday is a joyful one — for all of us."

Rapunzel couldn't agree more. Surrounded by her warm, loving family, in front of the crackling fire, she could not imagine a better Christmas.

Rapunzel sighed happily and flopped down next to Flynn on a cosy sofa. "Thank you. For all of this," she said.

"I should really be thanking you," Flynn admitted. "You know, this is my first Christmas with a real family. All those years I spent growing up in an orphanage, I knew what Christmas was supposed to be like, but it somehow never felt that merry. Until now."

Flynn and Rapunzel sat together in front of the fire, waiting for Christmas to come. But before long, Rapunzel fell asleep.

Flynn smiled. After all those spooky, sleepless Christmas Eves in the tower, Rapunzel had certainly earned a peaceful holiday. It had been a wonderful Christmas Eve, and there would be many more like it for years to come.

Bambi

The Wonderful Winter Tree

Bambi awoke one morning to find that the whole world was covered in a soft white blanket.

"What is it, Mother?" Bambi asked as he gazed around.

"This is snow," his mother told him. "It means winter is upon us."

"Snow!" said Bambi. He took a cautious step ... and then another ... and another. He felt the icy crystals crunch beneath his hooves and they glittered in the low winter sun. When he glanced back over his shoulder, he could see a set of tiny tracks.

"I like snow!" Bambi said, looking at the pattern his hooves had made.

"Snow is pretty to look at," his mother told him, "but it makes winter hard for all the animals."

Bambi was about to ask her why winter was harder than other seasons, when his friend Thumper came hopping over.

"Hiya, Bambi!" said the bunny. "Come on, let's go sliding." He led Bambi to the pond, which was frozen solid.

Thumper slapped at the ice with his foot. "Come on, it's all right," he told Bambi. "See – the water's stiff!"

Bambi spotted a black and white striped animal watching them from beneath the snowy branches of a tree. It was Flower, the skunk!

"You want to come sliding?" Bambi called, running over. "Thumper says the water's stiff."

Flower shook his head. "No, thanks. I'm off to my den. I'm going to sleep through the winter." He yawned. "Goodbye, Bambi," he said.

"'Bye, Flower," said Bambi. Then he spied another friend, a squirrel, scurrying up an oak tree.

"The pond is stiff, Squirrel," called Bambi. "Want to come sliding with me?"

"Thanks," replied the squirrel as he ducked into a hollow, "but I have to store nuts for the long winter." He showed Bambi the pile he had already collected. "No sliding for me today."

All these other animals seemed to be taking winter very seriously. So, Bambi headed back to Thumper and the frozen pond by himself.

Wheeeee! Thumper was sliding across the ice with some of his sisters. They made it look so easy. Maybe Bambi could skate, too? But when he stepped on the ice, his long legs lost their balance straight away. His hooves slid off in four different directions!

"Kind of wobbly, aren't ya?" said Thumper, skating around him. He laughed. "Come on, Bambi. You can do it!"

Bambi wasn't so sure. Sliding across the stiff water wasn't as much fun for a deer as it was for rabbits. His legs were long and he had further to fall!

His stomach growled and he realized all this running about in the snow had made him hungry. He said goodbye to the bunnies and went back to find his mother.

"Mother, I'm hungry," Bambi told her.

In the spring, summer and autumn, they had been able to find food almost anywhere they looked. Now that it was winter, Bambi could see that finding food wasn't so easy. There were no leaves on the trees and the grass was covered with snow and ice. His mum was right. This beautiful blanket of snow hid the rest of the world from sight and nothing could grow.

The snow was so cold that when he poked through it, Bambi thought his nose might freeze. For the first time, he noticed how cold he was and his whole body shivered. No wonder Flower had gone back den.

"Come, quick!" Bambi's mother called to him. She'd uncovered a small patch of grass and Bambi nibbled it eagerly.

At last, with his tummy almost full, Bambi could curl up with his mother for a nap. The ground was hard and cold, and the wind was chilly. Bambi was grateful to have his mother's soft flanks there to keep him warm.

"Is this why the birds fly south and why our other friends sleep through the winter?" Bambi asked her.

His mother nodded and snuggled even closer. "Don't worry, Bambi," she told him. "Winter doesn't last forever."

By the end of December, there was nothing left in the forest for Bambi to eat but bitter bark. The days grew short and the nights grew long, and throughout them, Bambi's stomach rumbled. Then one day, something truly amazing happened.

Thumper was the first to see it. "Hey, Bambi!" he called. "Would you look at that tree!"

Bambi followed the direction of Thumper's paw. He could not believe his eyes.

There, before them, was a tall pine tree unlike any Bambi had ever seen. It was draped with strings of bright berries and yummy popcorn, and from the end of each branch hung a ripe, juicy apple. Bambi thought that the most wonderful thing of all was the shiny gold star at the very top.

"Mother!" exclaimed Bambi. "Look what Thumper found!"

Slowly and cautiously, his mother drew closer. "It can't be..." she whispered. "It seems almost too good to be true."

"What is it, Mother?" Bambi asked her.

"The most beautiful tree in the world," she answered, circling it. She smiled down at Bambi, her eyes brimming with happiness. "What a special gift to have on your first Christmas."

"Who left it, Mother?" Bambi asked. He'd never seen anything like this before.

"I don't know," she replied.

"Maybe someone who loves animals," Thumper said, hopping up and down. "This is the best gift ever." He took a big sniff of one of the apples hanging low to the ground and wiggled his little white tail with pleasure.

"Can we share this food with every one of our friends, Mother?" Bambi asked.

"Yeah, and with my sisters, too?" Thumper chimed in.

"I don't see why not," Bambi's mother said. "Christmas is a time to share what we have with those we love."

Bambi and Thumper danced happily around the tree.

"Look at all the popcorn and berries!" Thumper cried. "And look at that star at the tippy-top, too!"

Bambi stopped prancing. He looked up at the golden star at the top of the tree. Then he glanced at the sky. The sun was just beginning to go down. He knew that very soon, there would be a star twinkling in the sky just like the one at the top of the tree. A gentle hush fell over the clearing.

He danced back over to his mother and took a big bite out of one of the juicy green apples. *Mmm!* he thought. Nothing had ever tasted so good!

Gazing up at the star and at the beautiful winter tree, Bambi could feel a happy, warm glow swelling inside him. There was enough food on the tree to feed all the animals who were hungry. *What a magical gift*, thought Bambi. Winter was long and hard ... and yet it could be wonderful, after all.

Pinocchio

The Perfect Gift

Christmas was just a few days away. Geppetto, the old wood-carver, was busy in his workshop, making toy soldiers and pretty dolls for the boys and girls in the village. There seemed to be more toys than usual to carve and paint this year. *I hope I get all the dolls made in time*, he thought, working as quickly as he could.

Geppetto's son, Pinocchio, wanted to help his father. He knew that Geppetto worked harder during the Christmas season than at any other time of the year.

While Geppetto worked day and night with his carving knife and paint brushes, Pinocchio had other ideas. He couldn't make toys, but he could make their home ready for the Christmas holidays.

He asked his friend, Jiminy Cricket, to help him decorate the house. They put up a tree and strung popcorn on its branches. They even hung prickly garlands of holly. All to surprise his dad!

This would be Pinocchio's first Christmas as a real boy, so he wanted it to be special.

"Jiminy," Pinocchio said, "I want to find the perfect gift for Geppetto. He should have something special. Will you help me?"

"Hmm," Jiminy said. "Well, if you ask me —"

"Maybe he would like a new knife to carve with?" Pinocchio said. Though he worried he might not have enough money for that. "What about some warm gloves? He could use them when he goes out on cold nights to deliver his toys."

"You know, Pinocchio, I wonder if a better gift would be —" Jiminy began.

"Socks!" Pinocchio cried. "Or a new hat! Come on, Jiminy, let's go to the shops and see what we can find." Pinocchio hurried out the door. Jiminy had to run to keep up.

In the shops, Pinocchio looked at socks, warm hats, gloves, scarves and even a warm woollen coat. Everything was too small, too expensive, or too ordinary. Pinocchio wanted to find something special.

By Christmas Eve, Pinocchio still hadn't found the perfect gift for Geppetto. He couldn't help feeling sad.

"What am I going to do?" he asked Jiminy.

"Well, I do have this idea," the cricket said.

"Really?" Pinocchio asked. "Please tell me!"

Jiminy sat him at the table and handed him a quill pen.

"You want to give your father something he really needs?"

"I sure do." Pinocchio beamed.

"Write this," Jiminy said. "'Dear Geppetto, my gift to you is an extra pair of hands and an extra-willing heart. Love, Pinocchio.'"

When Pinocchio finished writing, he looked up at Jiminy. "Now what?" he asked.

"Now, you put the note in here." Jiminy held out a box. Pinocchio dropped the note in. Then, Jiminy wrapped the package with bright paper and a big bow.

"Geppetto will be very happy with this gift," Jiminy said.

"But it's just a scrap of paper," Pinocchio said. "What sort of a gift is that?"

Jiminy smiled. "You might be surprised."

Geppetto took a break from his work to share a Christmas Eve dinner with his son. After the meal, Pinocchio presented Geppetto with his gift.

"What's this?" he asked.

"Your Christmas present," Pinocchio replied. "I hope you like it."

Geppetto untied the bow and tore the wrapping paper away.

"Why ... this is the perfect present!" he cried. "I could use an extra pair of hands in my workshop. How did you know, Pinocchio?"

Pinocchio smiled. Jiminy had been right – he was surprised at how much joy his simple gift brought to his father.

"I'm glad to help," Pinocchio said. "I can start right now if you want."

Pinocchio cleared away the dinner dishes from the table, washed them and put them away. Then, he went to Geppetto's workshop. He swept up the wood shavings, and boxed and wrapped the new toys. He made labels for each box so that Geppetto would know which child each gift was for.

The two of them made the perfect team!

When Geppetto set out to deliver the last of the gifts, Pinocchio went up to bed. He was tired after helping his father all night. But he couldn't ignore the warm feeling in his tummy – he was pleased to have made his father so happy. As he drifted off to sleep, he promised himself that he would help out more often.

That night, the Blue Fairy appeared.

"Because you have been so thoughtful this year, I have come to grant you one very special Christmas wish," she said. "Think carefully about what you want."

Pinocchio thought about the many wishes he could ask for. But he still only wanted one thing.

"I want to give Geppetto the perfect Christmas gift," he told the Blue Fairy. "Something that he will love forever."

The Blue Fairy smiled. She knew just what the perfect present would be. "You are a very kind and loving boy, Pinocchio," she said. "I'm sure Geppetto will treasure this gift for years to come."

The next morning, Geppetto woke up early. He tiptoed downstairs to light the fire. He was so happy that Pinocchio had helped him the night before, that he wanted to surprise his son. It was his greatest wish to make Pinocchio's first Christmas special.

Geppetto went to place his gifts for Pinocchio under the tree. He had carved a beautiful toy rocking horse and had crafted a playful jack-in-the-box. When he looked at the tree, he gasped.

A wooden puppet hung from the branches. It wore a pair of red dungarees and a red feather in its cap. It looked just like his son!

"My dear Pinocchio!" Geppetto said with a smile.

He examined the puppet, lifting its arms and legs. It looked just like a puppet he had made a long time ago....

He thought back to the lonely night when he had made a wish on the Wishing Star. He'd hoped that the puppet he was making would turn into a real boy. A boy he could love. The Blue Fairy had granted his wish, and Pinocchio the wooden puppet had turned warm and loving. He'd become Geppetto's son.

When Pinocchio heard his father moving about, he and Jiminy ran downstairs as fast as they could.

"Merry Christmas," he cried.

Geppetto sat in his favourite chair, holding the puppet. "My gift! How did you make it?"

Pinocchio stared at the copy of the puppet. He'd been just like that once. He smiled. The Blue Fairy had chosen the perfect present for his father.

"Puppet Pinocchio was my favourite creation," Geppetto said. "Oh, how I've missed him."

Pinocchio felt a frown appear on his face. "You have?" he asked. "Have I disappointed you?"

Geppetto laughed. "Not at all, son. You've been perfect in every way. This toy reminds me of how very much I wanted a real son. He reminds me of how happy I am to have you."

Pinocchio smiled as relief flooded his body. He went over to the puppet and looked at it closely. It was like looking into a mirror! The puppet had the same dark hair and blue eyes that he did.

Geppetto stood up and started dancing with the puppet and singing. Pinocchio clapped along. *Father is so happy!* thought Pinocchio.

Stopping to catch his breath, Geppetto looked at his son and said, "No one has ever thought to give me a toy of my own to play with because I'm a toy maker. You understand how much I love toys, Pinocchio. Thank you, son."

"See," Jiminy whispered to Pinocchio, "I told you that you would be surprised, and now you've been surprised twice!"

Pinocchio nodded as he watched his father dance with the puppet some more. Then, he went over and danced beside the puppet that looked so much like him.

Geppetto held out the strings for Pinocchio so that he could try to make the puppet dance for himself. It was difficult, because the puppet was the same size as Pinocchio, but he didn't care. He was happy to share this moment with his father.

A little later, Pinocchio opened the gifts that Geppetto had placed under the tree for him. He laughed as the jack-in-the-box popped up and he rocked the small wooden horse across the floor. But the best present that he'd received had come from the Blue Fairy. He would never forget the smile that lit up his father's face. He hoped that they would share many more happy holidays together!

DUMBO

The Best Christmas

One December morning, Dumbo the flying elephant woke up to find the circus grounds strangely quiet. He stuck his head outside his tent. Where was everyone?

Then Timothy Mouse appeared. "It's the Christmas holiday," he announced. "Time to sleep late, play in the snow and get ready for all the celebrations!"

Dumbo looked puzzled. What was Timothy talking about?

"Aw, don't tell me you've never heard of Christmas before," Timothy said in disbelief. "Hey, fellas," he called up to the crows, "come on down here. I need help explaining Christmas to Dumbo."

The birds gathered around the elephant and began to chatter all at once.

"Why, Christmas is packages wrapped up in shiny paper."

"Now wait a minute! What about fancy holiday food?"

"Don't forget a big tree covered in ornaments and lights."

"And music! You can't have Christmas without carols!"

"Now do you understand?" Timothy asked Dumbo.

The elephant shook his head. He was even more confused.

"Hmmm," Timothy said, "this is gonna be harder than I thought." He and the crows huddled together and quickly came up with a new plan.

"Dumbo," said Timothy, "forget telling you about Christmas, we're gonna show you!"

Timothy Mouse scampered up onto Dumbo's cap. "Get ready for take-off!" he cried.

The crows took to the sky. Dumbo flapped his ears, heaving himself into the air to follow right behind them. They flew and flew and flew until, finally, a magnificent skyline came into view.

"Welcome to New York City!" Timothy announced. "I can't think of a more Christmassy place – except maybe the North Pole!" Timothy had grown up in New York and he thought it was the best place on Earth.

The little mouse gave Dumbo a tour of the bustling city, starting with the most festive place in New York.

"That's Rockefeller Centre," Timothy pointed out as they flew over a large tree.

Below, ice skaters glided and twirled around a sparkling outdoor rink. Dumbo couldn't take his eyes off the enormous tree, covered from top to bottom in twinkling lights and pretty decorations.

Timothy could tell that Dumbo was impressed. "What did I tell you?" the mouse asked. "People here don't just deck the halls – they decorate everything!"

Dumbo looked at all the people on the streets, full of holiday cheer. Some carried brightly wrapped packages. Some were singing carols. Everyone gazed up at the great big tree.

The sights and sounds of Christmas made Dumbo's heart fill with happiness. Now, he couldn't wait to find out more about the holiday!

Timothy Mouse and Dumbo flew down Fifth Avenue, where the shop windows were filled with beautiful Christmas displays. Dumbo watched the shoppers hurrying around with large bags of presents.

Timothy saw something else.

"Hmm, that's strange," he said. "People keep leaving presents in a box in front of that store over there. Come on, let's go and find out what's going on."

When Dumbo swooped down closer to the crowd, everyone cheered. They had never seen a flying elephant before. Dumbo felt like he was performing in one of his shows.

"What are the presents for?" Timothy Mouse asked a woman. "Is it the store's birthday or something?"

The woman chuckled. Then she explained that the packages were toys for children.

"There's just one problem," she continued. "The snow has slowed down traffic and I don't know how we're going to make all our deliveries on time. The boys and girls will be so disappointed if they don't get their presents this year!"

Timothy looked at Dumbo. Dumbo looked at Timothy. "Are you thinking what I'm thinking?" the mouse asked.

Dumbo nodded enthusiastically.

"Lady," said Timothy, "Dumbo and I would be happy to help spread a little Christmas cheer. I know this city like the back of my hand, and Dumbo here never needs to worry about stuff like traffic. You can consider those presents as good as delivered!"

The people on the sidewalk cheered. "Thank you, Dumbo," one man said. "I knew Santa had flying reindeer, but I didn't know he had a flying elephant!"

"Shhh," Timothy replied with a mischievous wink. "It's supposed to be a secret!"

Dumbo was given a sack of presents and a list of names and addresses.

"Ho, ho, ho!" Timothy called out as he and Dumbo flew off into the sky.

The pair arrived at their first stop. Through the window, they could see children hanging stockings over the fireplace. When they saw Dumbo and Timothy Mouse they shouted with joy. Timothy handed each child a brightly wrapped present.

"Thank you!" they cried as Dumbo and Timothy flew away. "And Merry Christmas!"

Dumbo and Timothy flew from one house to another. They dropped off dolls and dump trucks, books and building blocks, puppets and puzzles. Every once in a while, the crows took a break from sightseeing to pitch in and sing some Christmas music. They were the funniest carol singers that the kids had ever seen!

Timothy's favourite part was watching the children and their parents when they spied Dumbo outside their windows. They'd blink and rub their eyes, wondering if what they were seeing could possibly be real.

"What's the matter?" Timothy would say playfully. "Haven't you ever seen a flying elephant before?" Then he'd laugh.

Dumbo loved the way that the children's faces lit up when he gave them their presents. It made him feel happy right down to his toes.

"We'll come back to visit them again soon, Dumbo," said Timothy as they headed home. "I promise."

Back at the circus grounds, Timothy and Dumbo settled down for the night. Dumbo was exhausted from making all the deliveries.

"So, Dumbo," Timothy asked, "now do you know what Christmas is all about?"

Dumbo wasn't listening, though. He was thinking of all the children he had met that day and how he and Timothy had made them smile. It had been the best Christmas.

Seeing Dumbo's happy expression, Timothy said, "Yup, I think you do."

The two tired friends soon fell fast asleep. That night, for the first time ever, Dumbo's dreams – and his heart – were filled with the special magic of Christmas.

The Best Present Ever

"Hey, Lightning – look at me! *Woooo-eeeee!*"

Mater sledged past his best buddy, Lightning McQueen. It was wintertime in Radiator Springs. Christmas was just a few days away, and fresh snow covered the ground. The two friends were taking turns sliding down a snow-covered hill using Mater's one-of-a-kind junkyard sledge.

"I'm tellin' you, this here's the best sledge in Radiator Springs!" Mater cried.

"I know, you have told me." Lightning laughed. "Several times. It has its own headlights, superfast gliders –"

"And built-in bumper tyres!" the friends said together.

"Well, hold your horsepower," said Mater. "Because it's gonna be even more fun when we take it sledging at Kersploosh Mountain!"

Kersploosh Mountain was a water park near Radiator Springs. For just one day a year, on Christmas, the waterslides were frozen over so that cars could go sledging down the chutes.

"Uh, Mater, there's something I need to tell you." Lightning looked worried. "Remember that Russian Ice Racers Cup I'm competing in?"

"Well, sure," said Mater. "The one in a few weeks."

"That's just it," Lightning said. "They moved it up to this week. I'm not going to be here for Christmas after all."

Mater stopped dead in his tracks. "You're not?"

Lightning shook his head. "I'm really sorry, buddy. I know I'll miss Christmas at Kersploosh Mountain. But hey, maybe we can do something else when I get back?"

"Yeah ... sure thing," Mater said, trying to hide his disappointment.

Later that afternoon, Mater pulled into Flo's V8 Café.

"Hey there, Mater," Flo called. "Want to try a sip of my new eggnog oil? It's guaranteed to fill you up with Christmas cheer."

"I could use some," said Mater. "I'm all out of Christmas cheer."

"Something got you down, honey?" Flo asked.

Mater sighed. "Lightning won't be home for Christmas. He's in some Rushin' Rice Cup."

"That's too bad," Flo said. "I guess you'll have to celebrate the Christmas holiday early."

"Yeah, celebrate early! That's a good idea," said Mater. Then he thought for a moment. "Oh, shoot, I forgot about presents. I've gotta get Lightning something! But what?"

Flo looked thoughtful. "Hmmm. Well, you're going to miss him while he's away, right?"

"Yeah." Mater nodded eagerly.

"So how about getting him something for the race, so he knows you'll be thinking of him? Like ear-mufflers? Or a snow scraper?"

"Or snow tyres! That's a great idea, Flo. I know just where to go!" Mater dashed off.

"Luigi!" Mater yelled as he skidded up to Casa Della Tyres. "I need your help."

Luigi smiled. "For you, Mater, anything."

"Those snow tyres," said Mater. "The ones that used to be in your front window. Where'd they go? I need to buy them for Lightning for his Crushin' Dice Cup!"

Luigi's smile faded. "Ah ... I can do anything but that. I'm afraid someone's already bought them. They just left a moment ago."

Sure enough, outside, a big truck was driving away from the shop.

Mater raced after the truck, finally catching up with him at the crossroads. Mater explained the situation, then pleaded with the truck. "I need those tyres for my best buddy's Christmas gift. I'll give you anything."

The truck sighed. "Sorry, but I've been dreaming of speeding through the snow with these superfast tyres."

Mater raised an eyebrow. "Fast, huh? What if I told you I had something that goes even faster than those tyres?"

Curious, the truck agreed to meet Mater at the edge of town. Meanwhile, Mater raced to his junkyard to grab his sledge.

"All right," Mater said when the two trucks met again. "I'll bet my sledge is faster going down that hill than you in those tyres. If I'm right, we'll trade. Deal?"

The truck agreed, and soon they were zipping down the snowy slope. Mater zoomed past the truck – and won!

The truck happily traded the tyres for Mater's sledge.

Meanwhile, Lightning was helping Sally decorate the Cosy Cone Motel.

"I feel awful," he said. "Mater looked so sad when I told him."

"Well," said Sally. "Do you need to do the race?"

"Huh?" asked Lightning.

"It's not part of your normal circuit," Sally pointed out. "I'm sure they'd understand if you didn't go."

Lightning's eyes lit up. "You're right. Mater is my best friend. And a trophy is just another trophy. I'm going to withdraw from the race and stay here for Christmas!"

Lightning raced home to call Vitaly Petrov, who was hosting the Ice

Racers Cup. Vitaly told Lightning not to worry – he could reschedule the race

for after the holiday.

"That works out great. Thanks, Vitaly!" said Lightning.

He couldn't wait to tell Mater the good news. On his way to see

his best buddy, Lightning drove

past a big sign for Kersploosh

Mountain. He suddenly had an

idea for the perfect gift....

The next day, Lightning and Mater exchanged gifts.

"Open yours, open yours, open yours!" Mater cried.

"Okay," said Lightning. "But, Mater, I have some good news that...." Lightning trailed off as he unwrapped the tyres.

"You got these for me?" he asked, looking up at his friend.

"Yeah!" Mater grinned from mirror to mirror. "If my best buddy can't be here for Christmas, then he'd sure as heck better win his Blushin' Mice Cup! Do you like 'em?"

Lightning was touched. "Mater, I love them. But...."

Mater was already ripping open his gift. When he saw the two tickets to Kersploosh Mountain, his eyes grew wide.

Lightning shrugged. "My race was delayed, so now I can spend Christmas with you, buddy."

"No way!" Mater exclaimed. "This is awesome! I can't believe we're going to Kersploosh Mountain on Christmas Day! Now we can take my sledge and ... uh-oh."

"Hey, where is your sledge?" Lightning asked, looking around.

Mater shuffled nervously. "Uh, I may have kind of, sort of traded it to get you them there snow tyres."

The two friends stared at each other. Then they started laughing.

"Can you believe this?" Lightning exclaimed. "We thought we were getting each other the perfect Christmas presents, but we ended up getting stuff we can't use!"

Mater nodded. "Yeah, but I'll tell you one thing, buddy: spending Christmas together is still the best present ever."

Lightning smiled. "Same here, pal. I wouldn't change a thing."

Mater looked at the gifts. "Well, shoot. What are we going to do with four tyres and no race, and two tickets with no sledge?"

A twinkle came to Lightning's eye. "Well, we may not have a junkyard sledge ... but we do have a junkyard. Mater – didn't your old sledge have bumper tyres?"

Mater bounced up and down. "Oh, oh! I see where you're going." He started racing around his junkyard, collecting scraps to build new sledges. "This is gonna be so cool!"

On Christmas Day, Mater and Lightning sat at the top of Kersploosh Mountain. Beneath them was a new junkyard sledge. Except this one was extra-special: it had two seats, flashing Christmas lights, double gliders and extra-large bumper tyres.

"It's Mater's Sledge 0.2, with double the sledging fun!" cried Mater.

"You ready for this?" Lightning asked as they teetered on the top of the slide.

"You bet," said Mater. "As long as I've got my good buddy with me, I'm as ready as I'll ever beeeeeeeeeeee!"

Winnie the Pooh

The Sweetest Christmas

One snowy Christmas Eve, Winnie-the-Pooh looked up and down, in and out, and all around his house.

He had a tree set up in his living room. It was decorated with some candles in honey pots.

Pooh looked at the tree and tapped his head.

"Something seems to be missing," he said.

He walked over to the window and peered outside. Then, he walked back to the tree and thought some more.

Suddenly, a knocking sound startled Pooh. **Rap-a-tap-tap!** He turned towards his front door.

"Maybe whatever it is I can't remember I'm missing is outside my door," Pooh said.

When Pooh opened the door, he found a small snowman on his front step.

"H-h-he-l-l-l-o, P-Pooh B-Bear," the snowman said as he shivered.

Pooh thought the voice sounded very familiar. He invited the snowman inside.

After standing beside the fire for a few minutes, the snowman began to melt. The more he melted, the more he started to look like Piglet!

"Oh, my," said Pooh. He was happy to see his friend where there used to be a snowman.

"Oh, my," said Piglet. Now that the snow had melted off him, he could see Pooh's glowing Christmas tree.

"Are you going to string popcorn for your tree?" Piglet asked.

"There was popcorn and string," Pooh admitted. "But now there is only string."

Pooh thought some more, wondering if popcorn was what he'd forgotten. But that wasn't it, either.

"Then we can use the string to wrap the presents you're giving," Piglet said.

Something began to tickle at Pooh's brain. It was the something missing that he hadn't been able to remember.

"I forgot to get presents!" Pooh exclaimed.

"Don't worry, Pooh," Piglet said. "I'm sure you'll think of something."

Soon it was time for Piglet to go home and wrap his own presents. He said goodbye to his friend and went back out into the cold and snowy night.

Pooh stood beside his tree and tapped his head while he thought. Where could he find presents for his friends? It was already Christmas Eve. Was it too late?

He thought some more. He sat down in his cosy chair. Then he got up and had a small smackerel of honey. He peered out the window and watched the snow fall.

Then he had an idea.

He still didn't know what to do about the presents he'd forgotten, but he knew where to find help.

"Hello!" Pooh called as he knocked on Christopher Robin's door.

Christopher Robin opened the door and smiled when he saw the visitor.

"Come in, Pooh Bear," he said. "Merry Christmas! Why do you look so sad on the most wonderful night of the year?"

Pooh was just about to explain about the forgotten presents when something caught his eye. He pointed at the stockings over the fireplace. "What are those for?" he asked.

"Those are stockings to hold Christmas presents," explained Christopher Robin.

"But Christopher Robin," Pooh said, "what if someone forgot to find presents for his friends? And what if that same someone doesn't have stockings to hang because he doesn't wear any?"

Pooh looked down at his bare feet, then back up at Christopher Robin.

"Silly old bear," Christopher Robin said. He took Pooh up to his room. They dug through his drawers until Pooh found seven stockings.

"Thank you, Christopher Robin," Pooh said. He smiled. He'd picked a stocking for each of his friends to put their presents in: purple for Piglet, red-and-white striped for Tigger, orange for Rabbit, yellow for Eeyore, maroon for Gopher and blue for Owl. He also had one for him to hang over his fireplace.

He hurried off to deliver the stockings to his friends. As he walked through the Hundred-Acre Wood, he thought about the presents he still needed for the stockings.

"I will get the presents later," Pooh said to himself. "The stockings come first."

Pooh stopped at each of his friends' houses. Everyone was asleep. He quietly hung the stockings where his friends would find them. Each one had a tag that read: FROM POOH.

When Pooh got back to his house, he climbed into his cosy chair in front of a roaring fire.

"Now I must think about presents for my friends," he said.

Pooh was tired from finding the stockings and delivering them to his friends' houses. Before he knew it, his thinking turned into dreaming. He was fast asleep.

The next morning, Pooh awoke to a loud thumping noise.

Thump-a-bump-bump!

"I wonder who that could be," he said. He climbed out of his chair and opened the door.

"Merry Christmas, Pooh!" his friends cried.

There on Pooh's doorstep stood Tigger, Rabbit, Piglet, Owl, Eeyore and Gopher. They were each carrying the stocking from Pooh.

Pooh scratched his head. All of a sudden he remembered what had happened the night before. He had fallen asleep before giving presents to his friends!

"Oh, bother," he said. Then he realized that his friends were all talking at once. They were thanking him for their gifts!

"No more cold ears in the winter with my new cap," Piglet said.

"My stripedy sleeping bag is tigger-ific!" exclaimed Tigger.

"So is my new carrot cover," Rabbit said.

"This rock-collecting bag will sure make work go faster," Gopher said.

Eeyore swished his tail to show Pooh his new tail-warmer. "No one's ever given me such a useful gift before," he said.

Owl told Pooh that his new wind sock would help him with the day's weather report.

Pooh looked at his friends. They were very happy with their stockings, even though there weren't any presents in them!

"Something very nice is going on," Pooh said.

"It is very nice, Pooh Bear," Piglet said.

"It's called Christmas, buddy bear," Tigger said. He patted Pooh on the back.

Then, Pooh watched in surprise as each of his friends put a honey pot in his own stocking.

"I don't know what to say," Pooh told his friends. He was thrilled by their gifts. Honey was his favourite treat!

"Christmas is a wonderful holiday," Rabbit said. "Especially when you have good friends to share it with."

"Yep!" Tigger agreed. "But I know how we could make the day even sweeter."

He looked at the honey pot in Pooh's hands.

An idea tickled at the back of Pooh's brain.

"Let's all have lunch together," Pooh said. He passed out the honey pots his friends had just brought him. "Christmas ... what a sweet day, indeed."

Lady's Christmas Surprise

It was the week before Christmas. Tramp and the puppies gathered beneath Jim and Darling's brightly decorated tree.

"You all know what holiday is coming up, right?" Tramp asked, his eyes twinkling.

"Of course, Dad," Scamp said. He was excited. Christmas was the puppies' favourite time of year. Lots of guests stopped by to wish Jim and Darling a happy holiday.

However, the best part of Christmas was the presents. The puppies got to help choose a special gift for each of their parents. They loved being trusted with two such important surprises.

"Do any of you kids know what your mother would like for Christmas?" Tramp asked.

"How about a steak from Tony's Restaurant?" Annette said.

Tramp shook his head. "We can do better than that."

"We need to give her something special," said Colette, "to show her how much we love her."

"Why don't you ask her what she'd like?" said Scamp, his voice muffled. He was chewing on a bow.

"We want to surprise her," Tramp reminded his son. He nudged him away from the presents. "That's the fun of Christmas."

"Maybe we'll find something on our walk today," Annette said.

Tramp thought that was a good idea. While Lady was taking a nap, he took the kids into town to look for the perfect present.

The village bustled with shoppers, their carriage wheels carving deep ruts in the snowy road.

The dogs rambled up and down the avenue, looking in all the shop windows. They saw sweaters, cushions, brush and comb sets, bowls and collars. But Tramp knew that none of these things were the perfect gift for Lady. He wanted to find her something special. Something that she would enjoy and that no other dog would have.

Tramp and the puppies kept looking into the store windows and they peeked at the packages that all the people were carrying. All they needed was one really good idea.

When the sun started to sink in the sky, Tramp turned to the puppies and said, "We'd better head for the alleys and dig something from the trash."

As they crossed the road, Tramp noticed something sparkling in the snow. It was much brighter than an icicle. He turned it over with his paw.

"Holy hambones!" he cried. It was a gold and diamond necklace!

"What a bunch of rocks!" exclaimed Scamp.

"What a good stroke of luck!" remarked Annette.

"Just the right size for Mother!" added Colette.

Tramp smiled and then scooped up the necklace with his mouth. They'd found the perfect gift. He knew it would look beautiful on Lady.

Suddenly, Tramp felt worried and dropped the necklace into the snow. It sparkled in the icy crystals. He frowned.

"What's the matter?" Scamp asked.

"This isn't right," Tramp muttered. Then he looked at his children. "Sorry, kids, but we have to return the necklace. It's not ours to take."

"But where would we go to return it?" Colette asked.

"Yeah, it was just here in the snow," Annette said. "How would we even find the owner?"

"I say finders keepers!" Scamp cried.

"Come on now, kids," Tramp said. "We can take it to the police. They'll know who to return it to."

With the puppies following, he bounded down the snowy street to the local station.

Inside, officers hurried around taking phone calls and writing reports.

"Stay close, kids," Tramp whispered to the puppies. "I don't want to lose you in the crowd."

Tramp trotted up to the front desk, with the puppies following behind. He dropped the necklace in front of the policeman in charge.

"What's this?" the officer said as he looked at the dog and then back to the necklace on the desk. He picked up the necklace and looked at the sparkling jewels.

Tramp panted and wagged his tail. The puppies stood eagerly beside him. Yip! Yip!

"You found it?" the officer asked.

Tramp nodded.

"Good dog!" he exclaimed.

The policeman took the necklace and began filling out his report while Tramp and the puppies watched.

At that moment, a woman rushed into the station. "Help!" she cried. "My necklace is gone! I'm offering a reward for its return."

The policeman smiled at the woman. Then, he held out the necklace. "Is this yours?" he asked. He pointed to Tramp. "This dog found it on the street and brought it here."

The woman gasped. "Thank you," she said. She scratched Tramp behind his ear. "How can I repay you?"

Woof! Tramp looked at the necklace.

"A new collar," she said. "That's it!"

She took Tramp and the puppies to the shop next door. Tramp walked up to the counter and picked up a gold collar with green stones that looked just like the woman's necklace.

"I'll take that one," the woman told the shopkeeper.

Christmas morning came and the family gathered to open presents. Jim and Darling sat back and watched as the dogs of the household sniffed each of the gift-wrapped parcels.

Lady tore open the wrapping on her gift. As the paper fell away, her face lit up.

"You shouldn't have!" she cried. Her eyes sparkled like the green stones.

Lady dipped her head as Darling reached forward to fasten the collar around her neck. As the collar snapped into place, she leaped to her feet and pranced around the room, hopping from paw to paw, with her tail erect. She was just like a show dog, wearing the best collar in town!

"I love my new collar," Lady said. "What a wonderful Christmas surprise!

But I love my family even more." She nuzzled Tramp and each of the puppies.

"Merry Christmas, Mother," said the puppies.

Together, they'd made it a very merry Christmas, indeed.

The Puppies' First Christmas

One winter evening, Pongo and Perdita were watching TV with their puppies when a rustling noise in the hallway caught their attention. The puppies jumped off their chairs and ran to the doorway.

They all watched silently as Roger and Nanny hauled a huge tree into the parlour. It was fresh and green and made the room smell like a pine forest.

"What's going on?" Rolly asked, turning to look at his mother.

"Don't worry, dear," said Perdita. "It's Christmas Eve. This is just the beginning!"

"Chris-mess?" Lucky asked. "It does look like a mess." He wagged his tail.

The parlour floor was covered with pine needles, boxes of ornaments, tinsel garlands and strings of small lights.

Anita was waiting in the parlour to help Roger and Nanny. The puppies looked on in awe as their human pets began acting very strangely. Roger hung shiny coloured globes on the branches. Anita was winding a garland around the tree.

When the tree was finished and the room tidied, Roger flipped a switch. The lights and shiny ornaments cast a magical glow about the room. The puppies stared wide-eyed at the tree. The humans had certainly made the tree very pretty – though they still didn't understand why they needed a tree indoors.

That night, when Pongo and Perdita tucked the puppies into their basket, they told them all about Christmas.

"It's a time when people show their families and friends how much they care for them," Pongo said. He explained how humans sent cards, baked cookies and fruitcakes and sang festive carols.

"It may sound strange, but you'll grow to love the holiday season," Perdita said. She nuzzled Patch, who let out a yawn.

"Especially the beef bones left over from dinner," Pongo added.

"Bones?" Patch said, perking up. His father smiled.

"And that's not all," Perdita continued. "On Christmas Eve, after everyone's in bed, people sneak presents under the tree."

"Presents?" all the puppies said at once.

"What kind of presents?" Patch asked. "Can you wish for them?"

"I'd wish for a new bed," Lucky said as he climbed into the basket that he shared with his brothers and sisters.

"Why do people put presents under the tree?" Pepper asked.

"Christmas is about giving," Pongo told the puppies, as they gathered round. "People give presents to their friends and family to show how much they love them."

"I wonder if we will get any presents?" said Rolly.

"Maybe," Perdita replied. "Anita gave me a collar last year."

"And I got a red ball," said Pongo.

"I hope someone loves us," said Penny.

"You are all loved, whether or not there are presents under the tree," Perdita said. "Now time for bed. Tomorrow is a big day."

On Christmas morning, the puppies woke at dawn. They creeped into the parlour. Sure enough, there were piles of brightly wrapped packages under the tree.

"We are loved!" Freckles cried.

The puppies dived into the pile of presents. They tossed the packages around and ripped and tore at the coloured paper.

"Christmas is fun!" Rolly exclaimed as he shook some wrapping paper out of his mouth.

Lucky pulled open a box. "Perfume?" he said, and wrinkled his nose.

Penny dragged a spotted necktie out of some tissue paper. "What do I need with more spots?"

Freckles held up a lace handkerchief. "What is this for?" he asked.

Just then they heard Roger's and Anita's voices in the hallway.

The puppies looked at each other in alarm.

"Let's get out of here!" Rolly said. The puppies scampered around the room, hiding behind the sofa, under the chairs and in the folds of the curtains.

The puppies trembled when they heard Roger's footsteps.

He stopped in the doorway. "What on earth?" he said.

Anita walked up beside him. "Oh, dear!" she cried.

"Perdita, Pongo," Roger called out. "Where are you?"

The puppies heard the click of their parents' claws on the wooden floor as they scurried towards the parlour.

When they came into the room, Pongo said, "*Woof!*"

And Perdita repeated, "*Woof!*"

The puppies looked at each other uncertainly. "We're in for it now," Lucky whispered.

Then they heard something very strange. Anita started to laugh.

Roger said, with a chuckle, "Looks like we had some help opening our gifts."

"Wasn't that kind of the puppies!" Nanny said as she walked into the room and saw the mess of paper and ribbon.

"I wonder where they've gone off to," Roger said with a twinkle in his eye. "Here, pups!"

"There are still so many boxes to unwrap," Anita said, shaking her head. "I do wish they'd come and help."

The puppies looked around at each other in their hiding places. Then, one by one, they creeped out from under the chairs and behind the sofa.

They gathered around the tree as Roger pulled more packages from under the branches. "Go for it, boys and girls!"

Yip! Yip! The puppies tore into the bright wrappings and the tangled ribbons. They crunched cardboard and rolled around in the crinkly papers. Patch hopped into an empty box to hide. When Lucky started to tear at the top of the box, Patch popped up with a playful, "*Woof!*"

Pongo and Perdita looked at each other. "Shall we join them?" whispered Pongo.

"This is their first Christmas," Perdita replied. "Let them have their fun."

When the puppies grew tired of rolling around in the wrapping paper, Anita brought out a large basket.

"Sorry we didn't have time to wrap these," she said. "But then...." She smiled. "Maybe you've done enough work for today."

She handed each puppy a squeaky toy.

From the bottom of the basket she pulled out two Christmas jumpers for Pongo and Perdita.

"Anita knitted them herself," said Roger with pride.

That evening, after Christmas dinner was over, the puppies were still full of energy. They weren't ready to go to bed.

"We like Christmas!" said Pepper.

"We like our toys!" said Rolly.

"We like tissue paper!" said Patch.

"But remember what we told you about Christmas?" Perdita asked. She nudged her children towards their basket. "It's a time for giving."

"It's also about forgiving," Pongo said gently. "You were lucky that Roger and Anita weren't upset that you unwrapped their presents."

The puppies' heads drooped a little.

"We're lucky we have two wonderful humans," Perdita said softly. "That is the best present we could ask for."

The puppies raised their eyes to their mother hopefully.

"We are loved," Penny said. She smiled.

"You are all, each and every one of you, very loved," Perdita assured her children.

"And that's what Christmas is really all about," Pongo said as the puppies drifted off to sleep.

THE END